OCEAN
ADVENTURES

DANGER IN THE DEEP SEA

KATE JEROME

EARTHAWARE
KIDS

For my kids, Lindsay and Eric—
two incredible treasures! KJ

EARTHAWARE
KIDS

PO Box 3088
San Rafael, CA 94912

www.insighteditions.com

Text © Kate Jerome, 2023
Illustrations © EarthAware Kids, 2023
Photographs © OceanX, 2023

Published by EarthAware Kids
A subsidiary of Insight International, L.P.

Created by Weldon Owen Children's Books
CEO: Raoul Goff
Publisher: Sue Grabham
Art Director: Stuart Smith
Senior Editor: Pauline Savage
Editor: Kris Hirschmann
Senior Production Manager: Greg Steffen

Illustrations by Francesca Risoldi

Special thanks to OceanX:
Vince Pieribone
Joe Ruffolo
Carla Lewis-Long
Mattie Rodrigue
Andrew Craig
Jessie Boulton

ISBN: 978-1-68188-908-5

Manufactured, printed, and assembled in China
First printing, May 2023. WNK2023

10 9 8 7 6 5 4 3 2 1

Welcome aboard! You're about to join Marena Montoya on an incredible adventure with OceanX!

OceanX's scientists, marine biologists, and filmmakers use cutting-edge technology to explore the ocean and share their discoveries with the world! Its fantastic ship, *OceanXplorer*, brings two submersibles, a helicopter, science labs, and a film studio to incredible locations to reveal creatures and habitats that have never been seen before.

You can find amazing **OceanX** videos, photos, and fascinating information about the world under the sea at **oceanx.org**.

CHAPTER 1
A DIGITAL DOOR TO THE PAST

"Marena, sometimes I don't even know why we're friends," Aisha complained.

We're not friends. We're BEST friends.

My inner voice was at it again. I never know when it's going to pop up. Luckily, it's just me talking to me—usually with a little attitude thrown in.

It was her idea to start this project. Not mine.

I had a poster that had been lying on my bedroom floor for weeks. I was in no hurry to get it onto the wall. But Aisha felt differently. She likes to get things done. She was currently dragging my desk chair closer to the wall so she could stand on it. I could tell by her noises that she was impatient with me for not helping.

Aisha let out a dramatic "Umph" as she gave the

chair a final nudge to the wall. I ignored it.

"Aisha," I said, not moving a muscle from my sprawled-out position on the bed, "you've got to look at this website! It has information on real ships that never made it to wherever they were going. Do you know there could be as many as three million shipwrecks lying undiscovered on the ocean floor?"

Aisha gave a long look at my cluttered bedroom floor. The wreck connection was obvious.

"Most of these ships sank long ago," I continued. "And most will never be found. But it says here there is now a better-than-ever chance of actually finding a few of these old wrecks—"

"Is this poster straight?" Aisha interrupted. Her voice was sharp. It seemed like a good idea to sit up and give her my full attention.

"Looks great," I said with real admiration.

Maybe I should think about splitting my allowance with her.

Aisha eyed her work and nodded in satisfaction. Then she stepped down from the chair and began slowly pushing it back to my desk.

"Okay. *Now* I can listen," she said, plopping down next to me on the bed. Since the chore was done, she seemed ready to move on. Aisha was like that. She never stayed mad for long.

"So what makes it easier to find these wrecks now?" she asked.

"Well, for one, the tech is better," I answered. "Sonar equipment makes better maps of the ocean floor. And underwater submersibles can dive deeper than ever."

Aisha gave a "Makes sense" nod.

"Also, there's this website," I said. "People are making digital records of old ship's logs and diaries and uploading them here—for the first time ever! That means you don't have to travel to the library or museum where the books are stored. You can look at them from anywhere in the world."

"It must take hours to go through all of those old ships' records and input the data," Aisha said.

"Yep, and it's pretty interesting stuff," I agreed. "You've heard of Blackbeard the Pirate, right?"

"Of course," Aisha answered.

"One of his big ships, called the *Queen Anne's Revenge*, sank off the coast of North Carolina in 1718. But the wreck wasn't found until 1996. And the state of North Carolina didn't say it was for sure Blackbeard's ship until 2011. It took that long to study all the things they found."

"A pirate ship … wow! Imagine the treasure!"she said.

"Yeah, well, I think they found mostly old cannons and stuff," I said. "Not much gold."

"Yet!" Aisha said eagerly.

She had a point.

"Sometimes gold coins can wash up on the shore many years after a wreck," I agreed.

"Imagine going for a swim and finding some of Blackbeard's treasure!" Aisha said. She loved a good story. "So have you found any new clues?"

"For what?"

"Missing treasure, of course!" Aisha's voice had that "Why can't you keep up?" sound.

When I shook my head no, she got a faraway look on her face. I knew what that meant. Aisha was about to drop one of her big ideas.

"So, imagine this. What if you discover a missing clue that unlocks the secret of where a long-lost ship might be?" she asked. "Then we could sail out on the ocean to that exact spot. We'll get one of those underwater vehicles to dive into the deep sea to take a closer look. That's when we'll find the treasure. Could be gold. Could be jewels. Then we'll become heroes when we donate it all to ocean research."

Aisha sat up on the bed, her face shining with excitement. I had to smile. Her big ideas were always so creative.

But she gets so carried away!

It really *is* weird that we're such good friends. Sometimes we can be such opposites. She dreams big and moves fast. I like to ask questions and take it slow.

"Come on," I protested. "Even if I discover a clue, how would we convince someone to take us out on a ship? And borrowing a submersible? Are you kidding? We don't even know how to drive!"

I was trying to make Aisha see reason. There were a million more questions I could ask her. But I didn't bother. The ones I had already asked seemed like deal breakers.

Aisha seemed lost in thought for a moment. Then her mood changed. I could feel her excitement draining away like air escaping from a balloon.

"When does Lucas leave?" she asked in a forlorn voice as she rolled on her back to stare at the ceiling. "I just can't believe he got the internship on the *OceanXplorer*!"

My mood shifted, too. It was a tricky subject for both of us. My brother was so excited about working on the big research ship that he never shut up about it.

Don't get me wrong. I was happy for him. But I

was also a little jealous that he was going on a big adventure without me. It was the first time we would be apart for a whole summer. Mom and Dad said it would be a good "test run." I guess that meant it was practice for Lucas to see if he could survive on his own before he went away to college.

But what about me? What if I don't like being the only child?

Aisha was bummed for a whole different reason. Although she was thrilled about Lucas's internship, she was going to miss him big-time. That's because she liked him. And not in the "I think your brother is nice" kind of way. I mean she *liked* him. Lucas didn't know, of course. But I did.

There are no secrets between best friends.

"He leaves in two weeks. But there's good news," I said.

Aisha raised her eyebrow at me. She wanted to know more.

"Mom and Dad have decided our whole family should fly to Miami to see Lucas off," I explained. "OceanX is going to allow all the families to tour the ship with the interns before they set sail."

"I hate you," Aisha said quietly.

I grinned.

"No you don't," I answered.

She heaved a dramatic sad sigh. Then she grinned back at me as she jumped off the bed and grabbed her backpack to leave.

"Just keep looking at the shipwreck website," she ordered. "I have a feeling about it."

I shook my head at my friend as she left the room. I loved her enthusiasm about a deep sea adventure. But there was no way I was going to find a real missing clue.

Was there?

CHAPTER 2
A MISSING CLUE

"I told you!" Aisha practically squealed in excitement. She grabbed me and jumped up and down in a pogo stick bear hug. "I knew you would find something! You ask the best questions!"

"Aisha, stop! It's probably nothing," I protested as I pulled myself away. School was just out and there were lots of kids around. Nearby classmates started moving toward us. They wanted to know what all the excitement was about.

I looked at Aisha in near panic.

"Okay, okay," Aisha could see I wasn't ready to share the news. "Let's ride over to your house so you can tell me everything."

I nodded in agreement. Anything to avoid being

questioned in public. As we pedaled down the bike path toward my house, I wished I hadn't mentioned anything to Aisha at all. Knowing her, she would want me to do something. And there just wasn't anything practical to be done.

"So let me get this straight," Aisha said as she poured popcorn into a bowl for our after-school snack. She settled into her favorite kitchen chair. "You're talking about a real Spanish galleon, right? One of those old sailing ships from the eighteenth century?"

Before I could answer her, Lucas strolled into the kitchen.

"Oooh, a Spanish galleon," he said in a teasing voice as he opened the refrigerator to look at his options. It was normal for him to mock us.

"Hey, Lucas," Aisha said, suddenly perking up. "Your sister might've figured out where a real shipwreck could be."

Lucas turned around with a yogurt in his hand. "Yeah, right. This I've got to hear," he said as he sat down in the chair across from Aisha.

Aisha smiled. I scowled.

"It may not be anything, Lucas. I've just been looking at some online records of lost ships," I said.

Before Lucas could ask why I was doing that, Aisha jumped into the conversation.

"Marena found this cool new website that's turning old ship's logs into a digital database."

Lucas spooned some yogurt into his mouth and waited.

"And you know how Marena is," she continued. "After studying that website, she found something really odd!"

Ugh. She set him up!

To his credit, Lucas just whispered the wisecrack under his breath. Something about "It takes one to know one."

Aisha ignored the jab and leaned over the table toward him. "Marena thinks people have been looking for a very important shipwreck—in the wrong place!"

Aisha stayed frozen in her pose. I could tell she was trying to send mind bullets to Lucas. She wanted him to be impressed.

PUH-LEASE! Lucas is paying more attention to the yogurt cup than to you!

Aisha must've realized the same thing. She sat back in her chair with a slight shake of her head. Then she turned toward me with a "Your turn" look.

Lucas looked up from his yogurt cup and squinted his eyes at me. I could tell he was weighing the odds. Was I about to say something stupid, or would it make some sense?

Fair question. I've been known to do both.

"Okay," I sighed. "Here's what I know. In the early 1700s there was the War of the Spanish Succession. You remember that one?"

"Sure, we studied it," Lucas said as he stood up to toss his empty yogurt cup into the recycling bin. "It was a fight between some European countries. They were arguing about who would rule Spain after its monarch, King Charles II, died. But what does this have to do with a shipwreck?"

"I'm getting to that, Lucas," I said.

Don't rush me!

I paused to gather my thoughts, then continued. "As we've all learned in history class, wars take money. So Spain sent ships to its colonies in South America to collect gold and silver to pay for the fighting."

"They didn't just 'collect the treasure'—they *looted* those colonies," Aisha said with disapproval.

"That's another subject," I said, steering back to the point. "One of the ships was a Spanish galleon called the *San Luis Pedro*. In the spring of 1705, after it was loaded with treasure from South America, it set sail back to Spain. But it was an unlucky voyage. Just a few hours from port, the *San Luis Pedro* was spotted by an enemy English warship. England wanted the treasure, so the two ships had a battle at sea."

Aisha jumped in. "The *San Luis Pedro* lost. And it sank really fast."

"Yep, that's the story," I agreed. "And, although it's hard to believe, the *San Luis Pedro* and its treasure have never been found to this day."

Lucas was typing into his phone to fact-check my story.

"Hmm," he nodded, showing real interest for the first time. "It says here the *San Luis Pedro* was so loaded with treasure that it was a wonder it could float. Bet that cargo would be worth billions by now. So why hasn't it been found?"

I looked over his shoulder. His phone screen

showed an illustration of what the Spanish galleon had looked like.

"I don't know, Lucas," I replied. "Lots of people have been searching for it. For decades. They know when the battle happened. They also know the general area where the battle was fought in the Caribbean Sea."

"That doesn't make sense. If they know where it went down, then they must've searched that area pretty well," Lucas said.

"I'm sure you're right," I agreed. "But that's where it gets interesting."

I was warming up to the subject now that I had my brother's attention.

"Historians are entering new stuff on the shipwreck website every day," I explained. "At first I couldn't make sense of it all. So I decided to zero in on just the *San Luis Pedro* chat."

Could I possibly get any more nerdy?

Ignoring myself, I continued. "And I noticed something the other day. A researcher posted about an eastern flow found in the Caribbean Sea currents."

Lucas frowned. He had been studying Caribbean ocean currents to get ready for his *OceanXplorer* trip.

"That's weird," he said. "Most surface currents flow to the west."

Exactly.

"Umm, what difference does—" Aisha stopped mid-sentence. I could tell she was slowly piecing it all together.

"Oh. I get it," she said after a moment. "When you look for a wreck, you have to think about the currents because they would carry the sinking ship in whatever direction they flow. But if explorers thought the currents only traveled to the west, then they might not even look toward the east."

I shrugged my shoulders. "It's a possibility. I mean, there's got to be some reason they haven't found that wreck for centuries."

"I don't know." Lucas sounded doubtful. "Explorers do really wide searches of an area where they think a ship might've gone down. Especially with a treasure this large."

"Yep, all true," I said. "But that eastern flow is kind of a new idea. And I'm not sure how recently anyone has searched for this wreck. I also don't know whether they've used the latest sonar equipment."

Lucas nodded. "It's true that only twenty percent of the ocean floor is mapped," he agreed. "That's one of the things that the *OceanXplorer* is doing. Mapping the ocean floor, I mean."

"Do you think you'll get to help?" Aisha asked.

And … I'm done.

Lucas and Aisha launched into a full-blown conversation about his new favorite subject. I knew Aisha was willing to keep the questions going just to hear him speak. So I quietly left the room and headed back to my laptop.

I checked the *San Luis Pedro* chat stream. There were new entries.

Just think of all that lost treasure!

Yeah. That was the trouble. I didn't have any way to search for it. All I could do was think about it.

CHAPTER 3
AN UNUSUAL CHAIN OF EVENTS

"It's a big boat," Lucas said, staring up at the *OceanXplorer*. He didn't seem to want to move.

We were at the dock in Miami, staring at Lucas's new home. The ship was almost as long as a football field. It had a helicopter landing pad at one end and a huge crane to launch submersibles at the other end. We knew it had space for seventy-two crew members. And Lucas was about to be one of them.

My dad clapped an arm around Lucas's shoulder and gently steered him forward.

"Let's go take a look, son," he said.

My mom took my hand as we followed them up the ramp. She had a small smile on her face. The kind of

smile that said things were going exactly as she expected.

Mom is scary like that. She knew he was going to get cold feet!

I was feeling the opposite way. I would give anything to be going out on this research ship. I wanted to ask Lucas if ocean exploration included treasure hunting. I was also dying to check the *San Luis Pedro* chat again to see if there were any new posts.

It's official. I'm obsessed with that website.

But I couldn't stop thinking about the shipwreck. I mean, we were just a few days' sailing from the Caribbean Sea, where the *San Luis Pedro* sank. How lucky was that?

"Marena! Look who's here!"

My mom's voice was loud.

She knows you're zoning out.

I snapped back to attention and saw Dr. Anna Knowles walking toward us. She was the science lead for the *OceanXplorer*. Anna, as she had asked me to call her, was also a mentor at the aquarium where Lucas and I volunteered. But I had only ever seen her on a laptop screen, and now I was thrilled to be able to meet her in person. Lots of introductions followed.

"Welcome, Montoya family!" Anna said with a big

smile. "I'm so excited to see all of you here. Lucas, you are going to love this internship. And you are just in time for the tour."

Anna's enthusiastic greeting was matched by everyone we met. We started up on the bridge with the captain. He explained the ship's navigation system.

Next stop on the tour was the ship's kitchen, which Anna told us was called the galley. We looked at all the storage rooms and the large ovens. It took a lot of food to feed dozens of people for weeks at a time when they were out on a mission.

Luckily for us, lunch was being served, and Chef Becca was in charge. She and her assistants had cooked up a feast.

"Scientists join us from all over the world," Chef Becca explained, "so we provide a lot of different food choices."

She wasn't kidding. In one day they could serve everything from falafel wraps and pomegranate seed salad to handmade pasta and pizza.

Lucas sat with all the new interns. I had to stay with Mom and Dad. Surprisingly, they didn't embarrass me once during the whole meal.

Maybe being the only kid WON'T be so bad.

As lunch came to a close, Chef Becca stood to make an announcement.

"Our cupcake-decorating challenge starts in five minutes. If you are interested, please come see me now."

Are you kidding me? Cupcake wars?

Mom smiled at my eager look, then gave me a "Go ahead" nod. I loved watching bake-offs and cake-decorating contests on TV. But I'd never been in one.

Lucas was shaking his head "No way." He wanted to get back to touring the rest of the ship.

As I put on my apron, my mom gave me instructions.

"We're going to keep going with Lucas. But we'll meet you on the dock at two o'clock to leave. Do you think you can get back there by yourself?"

I nodded my head yes and gave her one of my "Do you think I'm a baby or something?" looks just for good measure.

Mom rolled her eyes and gave me a quick hug. I waved goodbye as she walked off with Lucas and Dad.

Chef Becca motioned me over to the counter and smiled a welcome. There were five of us in the cupcake competition.

"To save time, we actually made the cupcakes this morning," she explained. "Your challenge now is to decorate them!"

Chef Becca seemed as excited as the rest of us. We could tell she loved her job.

"You'll each get two cupcakes, and the theme is undersea life," she continued. "You only have twenty minutes. So, ready, set, go! And may the most creative cupcake critter win!"

I studied the other competitors. I was the only kid. It could be a disadvantage.

Then one woman cheerfully said, "I think I'll just make my frosting blue like the ocean."

Did she not hear the word critter? *Sweet! I've got a chance!*

Chef Becca had piled lots of ingredients and decorating material in the center of the counter. I thought for a minute. Then I grabbed the supplies I wanted.

Luckily, my grandmother had taught me how to make a simple frosting the last time she made my birthday cake. I knew the recipe by heart. I just mixed powdered sugar, vanilla, butter, and milk. Finally, I added a little cinnamon. My *abuela* said it was the secret ingredient!

The next part was a little harder. But I zoned in on the task.

Before I knew it, Chef Becca was calling, "Time's up!"

My fingers were stained green from food coloring and my apron was streaked with frosting. My tongue was also a little dark from all the sample licks I'd taken. But mission accomplished.

Two green sea turtle cupcakes stared up at me with googly-looking candy eyeballs. Okay. The eyes were a little uneven. And the flippers? Well, they were a little floppy. But you could definitely tell they were turtles.

I think!

Satisfied, I looked around at my competition. Three of the other four entries looked about the same as mine. You could recognize an octopus and a sea star. Barely. And, of course, there was the one with plain blue ocean frosting.

But the fourth entry was in a class of its own.

Wow. That's art!

Two ordinary cupcakes had turned into beautiful rainbow-colored fish. There were lines of different-colored candies to make the scales on their

backs. And each fish had a perfectly placed candy eyeball with cute little fish lips.

Since I was the last to finish, I had to place my two turtle cupcakes right next to the beautiful fish.

How embarrassing!

At first everyone tried to be polite. There was a lot of positive head nodding.

C'mon, people! We all know who the winner is here.

Thankfully, Chef Becca cut to the chase. "Everyone gets an 'A' for effort. But Mr. Jonas wins first prize with his beautiful rainbow-fish cupcakes," she announced.

The winner accepted his prize—a cool OceanX hat. We all celebrated by eating a cupcake. I actually ate both of mine.

At least they taste like winners!

🐟 🐟 🐟

All too soon, it was time for families to say goodbye to the interns. Everyone made their way toward the ramp to leave the ship. I spotted Lucas as I was walking away from the galley.

"Hurry up, Marena," Lucas said. "They want all visitors off the ship now. I'll go with you to find Mom. She's waiting on the dock to say goodbye. And she wants to catch the hotel shuttle, which is leaving soon."

"Where's Dad?" I asked.

"He's still talking to the captain, but we already said our goodbyes. He'll be along in a minute. He told me he's going to head downtown to meet his old college roommate. He'll join you and Mom at the hotel later."

I nodded and started to follow him. Then it hit me.

"Oh, no!" I muttered.

"What?" Lucas asked. I could tell he was getting a little anxious. Goodbyes were tough.

"Lucas, I left my backpack in the galley," I explained.

He gave a little sigh. Like he was annoyed.

"Look, I'll just run back and get it," I hurriedly added. "So go say goodbye to Mom and tell her to go on without me. I'll find Dad and go with him into the city. It will be fun to see more of Miami."

"All right, Marena, but Dad will be coming by in a few minutes, so don't be late. You don't want to miss him."

We both turned to go in opposite directions. Then we both stopped and turned back around.

I looked at him. Then I ran back to him, throwing my arms around his neck.

"I'll be home before you know it, Ray-Ray," Lucas said, using my special nickname.

"You better be," I whispered. I was holding on tight. *Do you know how much I'll miss you, brother?*

Lucas nodded as if he could read my mind.

Then we broke the hug and raced off.

There was no one in the galley when I got there. I remembered that Chef Becca had said the only quiet time they had during the day came after lunch. That's when they took a break before dinner prep started at four o'clock.

Luckily, my backpack was right where I'd left it.

Ugh. Why am I so thirsty?

The Miami heat and too many cupcakes came to mind. I searched for my water bottle. But it was empty.

It was going to be a long cab ride with my dad into the city. I needed to get some water. I ran to the sink. But then I stopped. Could I turn on the faucets when the ship was in port?

What if I break something?

Then I remembered. I had seen boxes of water on the tour of the galley storage. Chef Becca wouldn't mind if I grabbed one to go.

I walked back to the refrigerator storage area. There was a heavy cart loaded with canned goods that hadn't been unpacked yet. It was now partially blocking the storage door.

I tried to push it away. But the cart weighed a ton and I couldn't budge it. I shoved the cart's handle back in frustration.

But the storage door was already open a little bit. Maybe I could just squeeze through?

I slid my backpack off to make it easier to get inside. Sure enough, I just managed it. I soon found the boxes of water. I couldn't help opening one to take a quick drink. Drained it. Oh well—Chef Becca wouldn't mind if I took one more. But just as I was reaching for the second water, I heard a metal "thunk." Then the door closed with a click.

Not good!

I scrambled to the door and gave it a push.

The door opened. But only a tiny bit. There was no way I could squeeze my whole body back out.

I tried pushing on the door again. And again. It just wouldn't budge. Something was blocking it from the outside.

This is bad!

I was stuck in a refrigerator storage room and the boat was about to leave.

This is really bad!

I yelled for help but the refrigeration machinery was really loud. And no one was in the galley to hear me anyway.

After ten minutes of pushing on the door, I sank to the floor. All of a sudden, I felt a gentle up-and-down motion.

Oh, no!

The ship was actually moving. Away from port.

I panicked.

What if no one ever finds me?

I ordered myself to calm down and think. Chef Becca had to be back by four o'clock to start dinner. So I only had about two hours to wait. Surely, she would find me. I took some deep breaths to calm down.

Wait. What if there's not enough air in here to last that long?

I quickly moved my hand closer to the door. Even though it was only slightly open, I could feel warm air blowing in over my fingers. Okay, I thought as I moved closer to the precious air. At least I can't suffocate or freeze.

I wrapped my arms around my knees and huddled in despair to wait. I could think of only one final danger.

What if I just plain die of embarrassment when they do eventually find me?

CHAPTER 4
HOME SWEET HOME

Okay. I didn't die of embarrassment. But it was close.

"I can watch her during the day, but she's going to have to sleep in a girls' dorm. Anna said you might have room?" Lucas asked.

Hey, I'm standing right here. I can hear you!

It didn't matter. Lucas was so annoyed with me that he wouldn't look at me, let alone talk to me. Luckily, the woman he was talking to seemed nicer.

"Of course. There's an empty bunk in my quarters," she answered as she turned to me with a warm smile.

"Hello, Marena, my name's Kira," she said. "I do a lot of the social media around here."

I liked the sound of that. Rooming with an OceanX influencer sounded cool.

"Come on—follow me and I'll show you where you can stay," she continued.

We went down some steps and into a narrow hall.

"You have to walk single file down these hallways, don't you?" I raised my voice a little louder, eager to prove to Lucas I was really there.

Both Kira and Lucas stopped in their tracks. Lucas cringed. Kira's index finger flew to her lips.

"SSSSHHHHHH!"

It reminded me of how my aunt "shushed" me when she was afraid I was going to wake my baby cousin from his nap.

"First rule," Kira whispered, "is to be extremely quiet in the halls. Some crew members are up all night working and they need to sleep during the day."

She silently pointed to a sign on a door that said, "QUIET PLEASE!—Daytime Sleeper."

I clamped my hand over my mouth and

QUIET PLEASE!

Daytime Sleeper

nodded that I got it. When she made a "C'mon" motion, I followed her on tiptoes—just to be sure.

It'd be just my luck to wake the captain.

And let's face it. I had been in enough trouble for the day. Make that for the year. I couldn't believe I was an accidental stowaway on a ship! I zoned out, thinking back to my rescue only a few hours before.

Chef Becca had returned to the galley right on schedule at four o'clock. When I heard the clang of her dinner pans, I yelled for help. She came running.

When she got to me, it wasn't hard to figure out the problem. Turns out simple physics had trapped me in the storage room. Before I squeezed into the room, I had pushed the handle of the cart back. But when I was inside the cold storage, the handle fell forward again. Because I had changed its angle, when it fell forward it wedged between the latch and the door. Since the weight of the cart was so great, I couldn't push the door back open. So I was stuck. I mean, *really* stuck. It took two people to push the heavy cart away from the door so I could get out.

So why hadn't anyone noticed I was missing? Well, that was just bad luck. Being stuck in storage, I couldn't connect with my dad as he was leaving the ship. Since he never knew I was supposed to leave with him, he didn't wait.

Bottom line? My mom thought I was with my dad. And my dad thought I was with my mom. Lucas just thought I was safely off the ship.

My parents didn't figure out I wasn't on land until my dad returned to the hotel a couple hours after visiting his friend. That was about the same time I was discovered on the ship. There was a lot of frantic ship-to-shore communication until everything got figured out.

And Lucas? At first he couldn't believe I was there. Then he got embarrassed and kind of mad. I couldn't blame him. I mean, who wants their little sister tagging along on the first big adventure of their lives?

What made it worse—at least for him—was that I had to stay awhile. The captain couldn't turn the ship around just for me. And it would cost too much to give me my own helicopter ride back. So everyone decided I should stay on the ship until it docked at the next port. Then I could get off the ship and fly home.

Puerto Rico, here I come!

I snapped back to attention. Kira had stopped outside a door at the end of the hall. She opened the door to invite me in. Lucas stayed outside.

I was immediately impressed with my new living quarters. There was a tiny aisle down the middle of the room. On one side were bunk beds with small privacy curtains. On the other side was a wall of doors. Probably closets. The room even had a small shared bathroom at the very back.

Kira slid open one of the curtains on a lower bunk.

Behind it was a cozy-looking bed.

"This is mine," she said proudly. Then she pointed to the curtain above. "You can sleep up top."

I just stared.

How do I get up there?

Kira nodded to a small ladder at the end of the bunk. "Go ahead—try it."

I tested my weight on the bottom rung. It felt sturdy enough. So I scampered up the steps to the top.

"Watch—" called Kira.

Ugh—too late.

I had already bumped my head on the ceiling.

"You okay?" Kira asked.

I nodded, rubbing my head to get rid of the sting.

"Everybody does that the first time," she chuckled.

I carefully crawled into the bunk bed and laid down on my back. There really wasn't room to sit up.

A little ledge by my head had a reading light above it. But I couldn't believe what was at the end of the bed. Right past my feet there was a TV screen.

How cool is this?

I automatically looked for the remote.

Again, Kira was a step ahead.

"Yep, each bunk has a TV. There are over 300 shows and movies you can watch. But frankly, I haven't had time to see a single one. We're all pretty tired by the time we get to bed," she admitted.

Not me! Can't wait until tonight!

"So you're going to need some headphones," she continued as she searched around in her own bunk area. "I think I have an extra pair here somewhere."

Unfortunately, I was going to need a lot more than headphones. I wondered if Kira had an extra T-shirt and some shorts. I was too embarrassed to even ask about underwear.

"Come on, Marena," Lucas whispered loudly from the hallway. "I'm sure Kira has stuff she needs to do. And I need to get to Mission Control, so you need to come with me."

Unfortunately, *somebody* had to babysit the stowaway. And both my parents and the captain had agreed that Lucas was the best person for the job.

It wasn't going over well with either one of us.

"Go with your brother," Kira encouraged. "I'll start gathering some gear for you so you can shower and change when you get back."

I felt myself starting to tear up at her kindness.

I feel so stupid about all this!

Kira squeezed my arm. "C'mon—it's not so bad. Just think of it as an adventure," she whispered. "You've already set a record for being the youngest deckhand on the ship. Who knows what else you will do?"

"So do we have to go see the captain again?" I whispered to Lucas. I had been following him up and down steps and hallways. This one looked familiar.

Does he even know where he's going?

"Why would you think that?" he asked impatiently.

"Well, you said we were going to Mission Control—"

"We are," Lucas said. "But that's not where the captain is—he's on the bridge, steering the ship. We're going below deck to Mission Control. That's where they direct all of the underwater operations. And, uh, I think it's this way," he said as he headed off in another direction.

I dutifully followed.

"And why do we have to go to Mission Control?" I asked.

"I want to watch them fly an ROV," Lucas answered.

"Lucas, you might as well be speaking a foreign language," I said in frustration, stopping dead in the hallway. "I give up."

"Marena, come on!" Lucas urged.

I didn't move. My stubborn streak had kicked in.

"I'm not taking another step until you tell me what it means to fly an ROV," I whispered fiercely.

It was a classic sibling standoff.

Realizing I wouldn't move, Lucas gave in. He took a deep breath and began to explain.

"*ROV* stands for 'remotely operated vehicle'," he said. "And when you fly an ROV, it just means you drive it around in the water. Kind of like a remote-controlled car. *Chimaera* is the full-size ROV, but they have a mini ROV, too."

"*Chimaera*?"

"Yes, *Chimaera*. It's named after a very cool deep-sea fish," he answered. "Of course, the ROVs are different from *Neptune* and *Nadir*."

"And who are they?" I asked.

"Not *who*. WHAT." Lucas sighed as if I knew absolutely nothing.

Which is true!

"*Neptune* and *Nadir* are the underwater submersibles that carry people. The ROVs do not carry humans."

"Oh. Got it," I answered. So *Chimaera* was the full-size ROV. And *Neptune* and *Nadir* were the submersibles. It wasn't hard once he explained things. But seriously. These things all have names? I thought of how Aisha would laugh at that.

Boy, is she going to freak out when she learns where I am!

I really missed my friend. In fact, when I had been stuck in the refrigerator storage room, I had had a few conversations with her. Just in my head, of course. It helped calm me down. That's because I knew Aisha wouldn't think any of this was bad luck. She'd think of it as an opportunity for adventure, or maybe even a chance to look for sunken treasure!

She may be right, too!

After all, we were headed for Puerto Rico. And according to the geography I remembered, the Caribbean Sea was just south of the island. I could almost hear the sunken *San Luis Pedro* calling to me. It was just waiting to be discovered.

"Marena!" Lucas sharply whispered my name. I snapped out of my daydream. He was motioning me forward. So I once again followed along. Eventually, we came to the door marked Mission Control. Lucas seemed very pleased with himself for finding it.

"The ROV controllers are over here," Lucas said as we entered a large room.

My mouth fell open as I followed him to one end of the room. The underwater vehicle control center felt like a cross between some kind of starship and a video arcade. A pilot and co-pilot sat in two big leather chairs. There were more than a dozen video screens in front of them. Each showed different pictures and data. The whole wall lit up with the brilliant displays.

"Bridge, this is ROV," the pilot said aloud.

"Good evening, ROV. Go ahead," came a voice in crisp reply.

I looked around for the source of the voice. Lucas saw my look and whispered, "That's the captain speaking from the bridge."

"Could we carry on at the same bearing with a speed of point five knots, please?" asked the ROV pilot.

"Affirmative. Same bearing at point five speed," the captain replied.

It sounded like a conversation between a control tower and an airline pilot. But in this case the control tower was the captain on the bridge. And the pilot was "flying" an underwater vehicle.

"They told us all about this on the tour this morning," Lucas explained. "The ROV is attached to the ship with a long cable. The pilot uses controls to fly the ROV up and down and in different directions. But the ROV can't get any farther away from the ship than the length of that cord."

"Wow," I said looking at the control stick the pilot was using. "It's just like the controller for your video games, Lucas."

He actually cracked a small smile. I knew we were both thinking the same thing.

Who knew that playing video games is valuable job training?

My attention turned to the chair next to the pilot.

"If the pilot flies the ROV, what's the co-pilot doing?" I asked.

"That's the really fun part," Lucas answered. "The pilot gets the ROV to a location. But when the ROV gets there, it sometimes needs to do something."

"Like what?" I asked.

"Well, maybe they want it to dig in the seafloor," he answered.

"You mean for buried treasure?" I asked.

Lucas rolled his eyes.

"No, Marena, to collect a sample of the different bottom layers. Or to pick up a piece of coral to bring back for study," he answered.

"So how does it do that?" I asked, feeling slightly disappointed.

"The ROV has two arms," he said. "They're called manipulators. The co-pilot controls these arms. Whenever he moves that handle in his hand, a manipulator arm does the same thing he's doing."

Amazing. I immediately saw how the ROV became not only the eyes but also the hands of Mission Control. But my questions weren't nearly done. There was a small table behind the pilot and co-pilot. Two people with laptops were busy talking to each other.

"And who are they?" I asked.

"Those are the scientists who are actually running the current mission of the ROV," Lucas said. "They design the study and tell the pilot and co-pilot what they want. Then the pilot and co-pilot fly the ROV to the right location and use the manipulator arms to get the scientists what they need."

The scientists, pilot, and co-pilot were all talking together as they watched the ROV make its way around the ocean floor. It was obviously a team effort.

Despite my interest, I suddenly had to stifle a yawn.

Lucas saw it. "C'mon," he said. "I'll take you back to Kira so you can get some sleep."

"But Lucas—"

At that very moment, the co-pilot seemed to notice me for the first time. It was almost like he heard my complaint. He took a time-out to introduce himself.

"Hey, my name is Colin," he said, holding out his

fist for a bump. "I hear you got onto the ship in a pretty unusual way."

Did everyone already know my story?

I nervously wondered what he thought about stowaways. But Colin's big grin told me I had nothing to fear.

"Yes sir—my name's Marena," I answered as I met his fist with my own.

"Now that you're onboard, you don't mind if we put you to work, do you?" he asked.

"Oh, no!" I quickly answered. "I'd love to help out!"

"She can help clean the decks and stuff," Lucas reassured Colin.

Lucas—come ON!

Colin noticed my nose wrinkling and grinned a little bigger.

"Maybe when you're done with all that, you can stop back into Mission Control," he suggested. "We could use a little help operating these manipulator arms."

"Are you kidding?" I asked, wide-eyed. "I'll definitely be back for that!"

Lucas stared at me for a minute. I read a few

different things in his look. For a minute, he almost seemed impressed. Then he just shook his head like he couldn't believe how lucky I was.

Frankly, I couldn't agree more.

Could all this really be happening? To ME?

CHAPTER 5
LIFE AT SEA

At the speed the ship was currently going, it would take about three and a half days to go from Miami, Florida, to the port in San Juan, Puerto Rico. It didn't seem like nearly enough time for me to ask all my questions.

I had wanted to watch a movie when I crawled into my cozy bunk last night. But I fell asleep before I ever got around to turning on the TV. Kira had to wake me up this morning. When I first opened my eyes I was confused.

Where am I?

Then the gentle up-and-down movement of the ship reminded me.

Wow. It wasn't a dream!

After I changed into the clothes Kira lent me, we headed to the galley for breakfast. By now, everyone on the ship had heard my story. There were a lot of high fives from the crew.

"You're quite the celebrity, Marena!" Chef Becca said.

I shook my head in protest. But as I bit into my nut-butter bagel, I had to admit that it felt kind of good to be noticed.

Each crew member had different jobs to do every day. Lucas showed me his printout. It was expected that I would share duties with him.

I eagerly looked at the list.

Any chance?

Nah. Treasure-hunting wasn't on it. But "needle gunning" was listed. I didn't know what that was, but it sounded fun.

I was wrong.

Turns out, needle gunning is a maintenance job. Since the ship's deck is constantly exposed to water and sun, its paint was always rusting.

Yeah. Same thing happens to my bike when I leave it out in the rain.

Anyway. Since rust weakens the metal, it has to be removed, and a needle gun is the special tool that does the job. It works kind of like the electric sander that we use to take the rust off the metal railings at the front of our house.

But that was only half the task. After you get the rust off, the spot has to be repainted. So Lucas and I were a team. He used the needle gun to remove the rust and I followed up with the fresh paint. It wasn't hard, but we had to wear a mask and goggles for protection. So it got pretty hot.

I didn't complain. It was nice to be up on deck where you could see the water. However, I was relieved when it finally came time for a break.

"So what's next on the list?" I asked. I had taken a long drink of water and was now slathering sunblock on my face. Eyes shut.

"Dolphins off the starboard side!" we both heard Anna's voice call out.

I quickly opened my eyes and looked to my left. "Where?"

"No, Marena, starboard!" Lucas said as he pointed to my right.

Ugh. I forgot. On a boat, *starboard* means "right side" and *port* means "left side".

Why can't they just call it "right" and "left" like we do on land?

Lucas and I ran to the ship's railing and looked over the side. A pod of bottlenose dolphins was racing alongside the ship. The dolphins' sleek bodies moved so easily through the water.

I leaned over the railing as far as I dared so that I could watch. Anna and a few others who happened to be up on deck joined us for the show.

"Why are they swimming with us?" I asked. "Do they really want to race?"

Anna laughed. "Dolphins are such curious creatures. They like to check out anything new in their environment," she said. "Sometimes we see them riding the wake of the ship on the bow, almost like surfing. We can hear them communicating with each other. It does sometimes seem like they are playing."

I could've watched the dolphins all day. But Lucas had to meet with the other interns, so we headed back to the galley. Luckily, I didn't have to go to the meeting with Lucas. Instead, he set me up with his laptop at an empty table. I really wanted to email Aisha. And of course, I couldn't wait to visit my favorite website to catch up on the latest shipwreck chat.

"Promise you won't move from this table until I come back," Lucas said. I could tell he really didn't trust me on my own.

"Promise," I answered. Chef Becca was bustling around in the background, getting ready for lunch. I looked her way and she waved.

"I'll be back in time to have lunch with you," Lucas said.

"Okay," I agreed. "But Lucas, can we please go back to Mission Control after lunch?"

But he was already walking away and just shrugged his shoulders.

He'll do it. He wants to go as much as I do!

I happily settled in to email Aisha. It was a pretty long one, but to my surprise, I got an immediate reply. She must have just been staring at her inbox. Good thing it was a Saturday.

Aisha was even more excited about my "very lucky chain of events" than I thought. She pointed out more than once that we were headed in the right direction to look for treasure. And if we were this close to the Caribbean Sea, where the *San Luis Pedro* was lost, she just figured I'd find a way to search for it.

Good old Aisha. She always kept the big picture in mind. But I was only supposed to be in Puerto Rico long enough to catch a plane back home. There was no way I was going to be able to search for treasure— no matter how close it might be.

CHAPTER 6
A DEEP SEA SWORDFIGHT

Lucas and I were in luck when we went back to Mission Control. Anna was leading the science mission. Colin was co-piloting and in position to use the manipulator. Anna nodded a hello.

"We're going down to collect a sample of the coral we spotted yesterday. We want to see how healthy the reef is in this area," she said.

I watched the screens. *Chimaera* was already on the bottom and its manipulator arm was out.

Colin motioned me over.

"Ready to give it a try?"

I eagerly nodded my head yes.

"Okay, just watch me for a minute. Do you see how I move this handle and the ROV arm responds?"

I could see how he made the manipulator arm extend. Then I saw how he opened and closed the clawlike hand at the end of the arm.

He stood up to give me his seat. Once I'd settled in, he handed me the controls. I pulled lightly to bring the arm up. It didn't move much.

"A little more firmly," Colin said.

I tried again and the arm swung wildly in the water.

"A little less," Colin coached. "Try not to overcorrect."

I made a steadier movement and the arm responded in a smooth motion.

Colin nodded his approval. "Now open and close the claw. See if you can pick up that rock."

I practiced the grabbing motion one time. Then I moved the arm carefully into position above the rock. I slowly lowered the open claw. It felt like an extension of my own hand.

I picked the rock up and held it.

Everyone in Mission Control whooped in delight. I had no idea they were all watching.

"You're a natural at this, kid!" the pilot exclaimed.

"He's right," agreed Colin. "Nobody ever gets it

right the first time. It usually takes people much longer to get the feel of that arm."

I was smiling in delight when all of a sudden, a big blur swept in front of the arm. It knocked the rock right out of the manipulator hand.

"What was that?" Lucas asked.

Before anyone could answer, the shape came back. It was a huge fish. And it looked like it had a long spear as a nose.

"That's a swordfish!" Anna said with excitement. "I'm guessing full grown by its size. Look at that tail and sleek body. It's just built for speed."

"It's a beauty, all right," agreed Colin. "But it's not happy with *Chimaera*."

Sure enough, at the next pass, the swordfish made a stab at the ROV with its sharp bill.

"It must think it's prey," Anna said. "You know this fish can swim at really high speeds. Do you think it can do any damage?"

Just as Anna asked the question, the swordfish came into view again. Although the fish was fast, everything seemed to go in slow motion as we watched it spear a hose underneath the ROV with its bill.

Alarms immediately went off. The big fish thrashed in fury. Oil began leaking from the hole it was making with its bill.

I automatically retracted the manipulator arm to get it out of harm's way.

"Good move, Marena," Colin said as he reached for the controls and I moved away to give him his seat.

"Let's see if we can pull away without hurting this swordfish," the pilot said as he expertly flew *Chimaera* at an upward angle.

"Boy, that's going to be a nasty hole in the hose," he added.

The mood in Mission Control was tense, but controlled. Everyone concentrated on their job to assist the pilot.

Lucas and I didn't speak. Our eyes were glued to the

screen as we watched the struggle. Then, as quickly as it had begun, it was suddenly over. The swordfish broke away and swam into the darkness of the ocean. By the way it moved, it didn't seem to be hurt.

For a moment no one said anything. We all looked at the hose of the ROV. How bad would the oil leak become?

But the oil wasn't leaking anymore.

Colin was the first to figure it out.

"Can you believe it?" asked Colin. "The tip of the swordfish's bill broke off in that tug-of-war. And now it's plugging the hole!"

We all stared at the screen. He was right! The swordfish had left a built-in fix.

"Easy now," the pilot said as he flew the ROV slowly back toward the ship. "Let's get *Chimaera* up for repairs while our luck still holds. Whew. That was a close one!"

We all breathed a sigh of relief. A happier mood came over Mission Control.

"That was the coolest thing I've ever seen!" Lucas exclaimed.

I wasn't yet sure.

"Do you think the swordfish will be okay without the tip of its bill?" I asked.

"I think so," Anna said. "Swordfish sometimes spear their prey with their bill. Most of the time, they are successful in the kill. But sometimes the prey gets away. And we've found bits of bill left behind before."

"Not a bad first day, Marena," Colin said, turning to me. "You really did well with the manipulator arm. And you learned the most important rules of exploration."

I did?

"Umm ... just to be sure ... what are they again?" I asked.

"Always be prepared for the unexpected," Colin answered. "And when the unexpected does happen, don't panic. Just think your way through it."

I solemnly nodded my head at his good advice. And for the rest of the day I couldn't get that one phrase out of my head. "Be prepared for the unexpected" kept ringing in my ears.

CHAPTER 7
NOT QUITE GOODBYE

The *OceanXplorer* docked in Puerto Rico.

It was a weird whiplash. A few days earlier I had been panicked—trying to figure out a way to get *off* the boat. Now I was just as panicked—but trying to figure out a way to stay *on* the boat.

"I can do any job! I'll even vacuum the toilets," I pleaded with Lucas.

I actually didn't know what vacuuming the toilets meant, but I had heard someone say it when she read her task list. And the way she said it made me think that it was not a favorite job on the ship.

"Ray-Ray, I get it," Lucas said. "And I'm sorry you have to go. But the captain doesn't have a choice. There are rules. You have to be a certain age. It also wouldn't be fair to others to give you a special spot."

I knew my brother was right.

"Cheer up. In a few years you'll earn your internship and be back here working on the ship all summer long," Chef Becca said as she hugged me goodbye.

I actually thought I had a shot at that. I had spent every spare minute I could working with Colin. He was teaching me so much. And even I could tell that I was getting really good with the manipulator arm.

As I trudged behind Lucas down the long dock, I took one last look over my shoulder. Anna, Colin, and Kira had also come to wave goodbye. Tears filled my eyes, but I didn't make a scene—just gave a small wave in return.

"Just think of how happy Aisha will be to have you home," Lucas said. He was doing his best to cheer me up.

If he only knew what Aisha really thought.

Fact is, my best friend was convinced I shouldn't come home. She thought I should tell someone that I suspected the *San Luis Pedro* shipwreck might be in a different area. With all that treasure at stake, she said, adults might be willing to listen to me, even if I am just a kid.

But it's just a guess right now. And I have no real evidence to support it.

I had to let the idea go. The faster I got on the plane, the better.

The cab ride to the airport was quick and easy. But the news once we got there was not good. There was bad weather in Miami.

"It's a total ground stop—no planes are allowed in or out," Lucas said after checking with the agent at the counter. "You're not going anywhere, at least until the thunderstorm passes through."

I could tell he was frustrated. He wanted to get back to the *OceanXplorer*. I didn't blame him.

"Let's go sit over there for a while."

He pointed to two empty chairs. The airport was getting more crowded by the minute. We were lucky to get them.

I nodded to the woman in the seat next to me.

"Are you on the flight to Miami, too?" I asked.

"Yes," she sighed. "I really wanted to get to Miami today, but I don't think it's going to happen. If this flight is canceled, there isn't another seat open until tomorrow night."

Just then Lucas's phone dinged as a text message came through.

He read it and sighed.

"Your flight's been canceled, Marena," he reported.

What? I get another night?

Lucas saw the hopeful look in my eye.

"Marena, you can't go back to the *OceanXplorer*," he said. "Remember, they're picking up another scientist in San Juan, and she has to take your bunk. There's literally no room for you on the ship."

Lucas got up from his seat, already speaking on another call. He turned and gave me a hand signal to "Stay" as he drifted down the hallway.

I'm not a dog, Lucas!

But there really wasn't anything else to do. So I sat and stayed.

"These are so good," I said between bites of the delicious side dish that had just been passed. "What are they called again?"

"Tostones," my host, Isabella, answered. "They are made from plantains—a cousin fruit to the banana."

Turns out, my adventure in Puerto Rico wasn't over.

I was still sad that I couldn't spend another night on the *OceanXplorer*, but thanks to the weather delay and my canceled flight, I couldn't leave yet, either. So after Lucas called our parents, he had talked to Anna on the ship. She had a good friend named Isabella who lived in San Juan. She offered us an overnight stay in her home instead of a hotel room. Lucas didn't want to leave me alone. So here we were on Isabella's patio, eating a lovely homemade dinner.

And it got better.

Isabella's uncle was having dinner with us, too. His name was Captain Jack, and he owned a shipwreck recovery business. Seriously. I couldn't believe I was having dinner with a captain who looked for sunken treasure for a living!

Aisha is going to love this!

So far, Captain Jack hadn't said much. He gave a polite nod when we were introduced. Sometimes he stared at his food. Sometimes he stared at us. Either way, it didn't look like he was up for a chat.

But it's your only chance!

Aisha would kill me if I didn't take it.

"Umm, Captain Jack, sir," I said. "Do you mind if

I ask you a question?"

His look said yes, he minded. But Isabella's frown at him said no, he didn't.

I made my move.

"I was wondering if you've ever looked for the *San Luis Pedro* shipwreck. The one that went down in the Caribbean in the spring of 1705?"

Before Captain Jack could answer, Lucas butted in.

"Oh, Marena, let Captain Jack eat in peace," he scolded. Then he said in an aside to Captain Jack, "Marena thinks researchers haven't been looking in the right place for the wreck."

Captain Jack put his fork down and looked at me. "Why?" he asked.

I felt my cheeks flush. Suddenly, I wished I knew a lot more than I did.

"Well, I've been watching a *San Luis Pedro* shipwreck chat on this website. And I noticed some people posting about a current flowing to the east."

Captain Jack continued to stare. He didn't say anything. So I went on.

"Since most currents flow to the west in the Caribbean, I was wondering if everyone knew about that one flow that goes east because—"

"You think the shipwreck might've gone more to the east than the west," Captain Jack finished as he picked up his fork and started eating again.

The way he talked about my idea made it sound like he'd heard it a million times before.

So much for your great hypothesis!

I poked at my tostones in embarrassment. Lucas squirmed in his seat. Isabella cleared her throat and made a slight movement. Captain Jack looked up at her in surprise. I actually wondered if Isabella had given him a little kick under the table.

"Well, you're not wrong about this, young lady," he said.

What? I'm NOT wrong?

I looked up in confusion.

Captain Jack continued. "It's just not a new theory. We've been considering the idea for quite some time."

Of course they had. What was I thinking? These shipwreck hunters were professionals. No way they wouldn't have been considering the eastern flow ever since it was identified.

Captain Jack could see by the look on my face that

I felt a bit silly. He glanced at Isabella.

"It's still a pretty good catch on your part," he admitted. "Shows you have a good head on your shoulders. So I'm looking for a couple of crew members to help on a short search expedition tomorrow. If you and Lucas want to join, you are welcome. There's no pay, but I guarantee you'll learn a lot."

Captain Jack had a way of saying things that made it sound like the phrase "and that's final" should be at the end of every sentence.

I eagerly looked at Lucas, but he was already talking into his phone. I broke into a grin when I heard him say, "Dad, Marena and I have a very exciting opportunity, and I called to get your permission ..."

CHAPTER 8
FULL SPEED AHEAD

After talking with Isabella, who would go on the trip too, our parents gave permission for us to sail with Captain Jack. Lucas then cleared it with Anna. Since the *OceanXplorer* would be in port for another day or two, she said Lucas was free to join Captain Jack's little expedition.

So early the next morning, we all made our way to Captain Jack's office on the dock. It wasn't that impressive. It looked like an old warehouse. Wind, waves, and salt air had given the wood of the building a rough look. For a minute, I wondered if it was safe.

That thought stayed with me when we entered. The whole place was a mess! Charts and maps covered every surface. Scraps of paper with handwritten notes were scattered all over the floor.

Was there a break-in last night, or is it always like this?

Isabella saw my look and smiled.

As if reading my mind, she said, "It's always like this."

In the middle of the mess, Captain Jack sat calmly at his desk. A beam of sunlight was shining through an overhead window like a spotlight on him. Tiny specks of dust floated through the light swirling around Captain Jack and his sea of papers. Two large computer monitors towered next to his laptop. Colorful graphs and data were changing in real time on their screens. Captain Jack was watching the monitors and scribbling notes on a pad of paper. He didn't seem to hear us come in.

Lucas and I looked at Isabella. We didn't know whether it was safe to interrupt to say hello or not.

"Welcome to CQ Explorations," she said. "Any guesses on what the *CQ* stands for?"

I'd say the "C" MUST stand for chaos!

Luckily, Isabella continued before I could say it.

"My uncle started the Curious Quest Exploration company more than forty years ago. As a young man, he was always asking questions," she said.

Lucas shot me a look.

Yeah, I know.

"Back then, he worked odd jobs around the dock and heard about shipwrecks that had never been found. To most people, they were just old stories. To Uncle Jack, they were a quest. So he decided to make it his life's work," she said.

"But has he ever really found anything?" Lucas asked. I wondered if Isabella would think his question was rude. But she didn't seem to mind.

"As a matter of fact, he's found three important shipwrecks," she said.

"Wow." I was suddenly much more impressed. "Were the ships loaded with treasure?"

My imagination was flying back to Aisha's big idea.

"Well, it depends on how you define *treasure*," Isabella answered.

Ummm … I'm talking about a treasure chest full of jewels and coins. What else is there?

"He did recover some Spanish doubloons that were worth some money," Isabella said. "But those gold coins just paid for the cost of bringing the shipwreck to the surface."

"So no precious jewels?" I asked with obvious disappointment.

Lucas frowned at me.

Isabella shook her head.

"I don't really think he's in it for the money, Marena," Isabella said gently. "It's more the adventure of it. He loves piecing together clues to find a ship. Then he loves learning every detail he can about the history of the ship and its sailors."

Isabella nodded toward a cluttered corner. "See that copper pot over there?" she asked. "My uncle considers that a real treasure."

Lucas and I looked. The pot didn't look special. Just old.

"It's a cooking pot. Over 200 years old," Captain Jack said. He had finally seen us and stopped his work to join. "It's one of five we recovered from an old English shipwreck. And it's a treasure because of the story it tells."

"What kind of story can an old pot tell?" I asked.

"Five big pots gives us an idea of how many mouths the cook had to feed," Captain Jack said. "There were probably a couple hundred sailors on that voyage.

Luckily for us, the heavy copper pieces survived in the sea long enough for us to find them."

I shuddered thinking of what—and who—did not survive.

Captain Jack was ready to move on. "So do you want to meet *Flipper* and *Jacques*, or not?" he asked.

I looked around, expecting to see pets. There wasn't a cat or a dog in sight.

"*Flipper* is the ROV and *Jacques* is the submersible," Isabella explained as we followed Captain Jack out onto the dock.

"What?" both Lucas and I said together.

We were shocked that Captain Jack had a ship with equipment similar to the *OceanXplorer*.

Captain Jack saw our looks and gave a shake of his head.

"How else do you think we're going to explore the ocean?" he asked.

Captain Jack's ship, the *Curious Quest*, wasn't nearly as big as the *OceanXplorer*. But, unlike his office, the boat was in great condition. You could tell the captain took a lot of pride in the boat.

"We've been hired to locate a cargo ship that went down in the 1940s," Captain Jack said.

We were all up on the bridge. Captain Jack had turned the piloting duties over to Ben, the Second Officer. The ship was headed in a southwest direction away from the island of Puerto Rico—out into the Caribbean Sea.

"What happened to it?" I asked.

"During World War II, German submarines sank a lot of cargo ships to prevent supplies from getting to the United States," Captain Jack explained.

"Would there be any treasure aboard?" I asked.

Captain Jack looked at me with a slight frown. He seemed a little disappointed in the question. But he answered me anyway.

"If we find her, I expect we'll get some airplane and truck parts. So yes, plenty of treasure," he said.

For a museum, maybe!

Lucas looked at me and shook his head. I folded my arms across my chest. I still didn't see what was wrong with dreaming about a serious haul of gold.

Captain Jack laid out a large chart. We could see a pattern of lines on it.

"This is the search pattern we'll use for the cargo ship," he explained. "We'll go back and forth in this tight grid so we don't miss anything."

I gave a small sigh. I didn't mean for Captain Jack to hear it, but he did.

"By the way, Marena," he said in a casual way, "I've researched weather patterns and have carefully studied the logs of the British ship that sunk the *San Luis Pedro*."

I looked at him in surprise.

"And based on that information, I would say that even though we're searching for the cargo ship, we may also be in range of where another big wreck might have settled."

"Captain Jack?" I said with excitement. "You mean we're looking for the *San Luis Pedro,* too?"

He gave a slight shrug of his shoulders and simply said, "That's the way of it. A treasure hunter is always searching for something special."

I heard the unspoken "and that's final" and wished that Aisha could be with us.

Who would believe we're actually living her big idea?

"So follow me," Captain Jack ordered us all. "No time to waste. We're almost ready to start the search."

We all followed him down to the deck below. No questions asked.

Captain Jack's Mission Control room was quite small compared to the *OceanXplorer*'s. There were only two monitors and two chairs.

Captain Jack immediately sat down in the pilot chair and put on headphones. He ordered *Flipper*, the ROV, to be dropped into the water. Then he directed Second Officer Ben on speed and bearing. The Captain was obviously an expert.

"Isabella," he said, "will you co-pilot?"

She slid into the seat next to him. I felt a little twinge of disappointment. At last night's dinner, Lucas had told Captain Jack how well I had done with the manipulator arms on the *OceanXplorer*. So I was secretly hoping for an invitation to try it here, too. But hey, what could I expect? I was still such a newbie.

As *Flipper* went down, we saw colorful fish. We even saw a couple of green sea turtles before the ROV got too deep.

I soon learned that the first thing you had to have in a search is patience. The ROV proceeded in long lines.

First, up one way on the grid. Then turn and back down the other way. Captain Jack and Isabella were constantly studying the sonar and video monitors. After a couple of hours, I was having a hard time staying awake.

Finally, Isabella said it was time to break for lunch. I couldn't disagree. My stomach was starting to growl.

"There!" Captain Jack yelled just then.

Startled, we all froze and looked at the image on the screen where he was pointing.

"ROV to bridge. All stop here," he ordered.

"Aye, Captain Jack, all stop now," came the answer from the bridge. We all felt the roar of the engines die as the ship came to a slow stop.

"Isabella, I'm going to fly *Flipper* down to the seafloor. Then I need you to pick up that object that looks like a rock," he said.

As soon as Captain Jack got *Flipper* in range, Isabella worked the manipulator arm. You could tell she had done this before. She grabbed the rocklike object on her first try.

But it wasn't a rock. As she lifted it up, it became clear that it was a heavy chain.

"It looks like part of an anchor chain," Lucas said.

"And it's an old one," Captain Jack agreed. "We may have something here." All of a sudden, Captain Jack seemed different. You could almost feel his energy rising.

"And I'm getting a reading on a large, square object about another arm's length away," he said. He turned to Lucas with an excited look.

"I've seen enough. Do you want to go down?" Captain Jack asked him.

Lucas looked confused.

"You mean … you mean in the sub?" he stammered.

"Well, we're going to have to go down about 500 meters to the ocean floor, so you certainly can't go without *Jacques*," Captain Jack said.

What Captain Jack said was true. Lucas and I both knew something about scuba diving from our work back home at the aquarium. We'd learned that even professional divers don't go much deeper than 200 meters on their own. The pressure from the water just becomes too great. But a submersible can protect people so they're able to go much deeper.

"Isabella can pilot and Marena can co-pilot," Captain Jack continued.

It was now my turn to be shocked. I looked at Lucas. I had so many questions! But Lucas's eyes were shining. Diving in a submersible was something he'd dreamed of doing, and I knew there was no turning back.

Captain Jack saw the look, too.

"All right, then. Let's go get *Jacques* and see what

we've found," he said.

I pictured a treasure chest full of gold and jewels from the long-lost *San Luis Pedro.*

Were we all about to become famous—and rich?

CHAPTER 9
DEEP TROUBLE

Captain Jack's submersible looked like the *OceanXplorer*'s—only smaller. It could fit two people—in this case, Captain Jack and Lucas—and it had a clear dome that allowed those inside to see almost all the way around them. *Jacques* was safe to 600 meters. The *OceanXplorer* submersibles, *Nadir* and *Neptune,* could go deeper.

"What's it like, Lucas?" I asked, adjusting my headset so I could hear his answer loud and clear.

"I think this must be what a goldfish feels like in its bowl," he said with a laugh. "I'm on the inside in my little bubble. But I'm looking out on a whole different world that is much bigger than I can see."

You could hear the wonder in his voice.

I couldn't believe my brother was diving for treasure.

"Wow—that's a lot of fish," I heard Lucas say.

I could see it, too. Captain Jack was piloting *Jacques*. But Isabella was flying *Flipper* near them, so I could watch the whole operation. *Flipper*'s camera was currently showing us a huge school of gruntfish swimming in front of the sub.

"How do they all know how to move together like that?" I asked. "Does a lead fish send out a signal?"

Isabella smiled at my question.

"Actually, there is no lead fish in a school," she said. "Each fish just uses its own eyes and a special sense organ along its body to keep a certain distance from the fish around it. When a school of fish move and turn together, it may look like they're following a big plan. But each fish is really just reacting to the fish swimming next to it. It's similar to birds flying in flocks in the sky."

I made a mental note to share this story with Aisha. *Maybe we could make a school of humans with our friends!* In the meanwhile, the submersible kept diving.

"It's getting so dark," I said.

"Yes, deeper means darker," Isabella agreed. Then

she pulled up a chart on her computer. It was labeled with different ocean zones.

"Scientists divide the sea into layers, called zones. They're usually measured in meters. There's a zone at the surface, called the sunlight zone, where light easily gets through the water," she explained. "But by 250 meters, you lose most natural light. That's when the sub and ROV need their headlights. Around 1,000 meters and below, it gets pitch black."

I looked at the deepest zones on her chart. One of them was called the abyss, which went as deep as 6,000 meters. The name sounded spooky to me.

"How deep does the ocean get?" I asked.

"Well, the deepest part is a place called the Mariana Trench. It's over 10,000 meters deep—that's over six miles down, if you're doing the math," she said.

I tried to imagine that depth. I couldn't.

"But the deepest part of the Caribbean Sea, where we are, is about 7,500 meters," Isabella said. She said it like it was no big deal. But it still sounded plenty deep to me.

When the submersible finally reached the bottom, it was about 500 meters down. Its headlights lit up a small path in the darkness for Captain Jack and Lucas to see.

"Look over there," Captain Jack said. The propellers on the sub were stirring up the soft layer of sand on the ocean floor. The headlights lit up pieces of rope that were beginning to float up from the loosened sediment.

"Maybe more evidence," Captain Jack murmured mostly to himself. He was concentrating on avoiding the rope as he steered the sub toward a wall of rocks.

"Let's see what's over this," he said.

The propellers whirred and the sub rose up from the ocean floor. As the sub inched over the top of the rocks, the video screen showed a sudden drop-off on the other side. It was a deep trench. And the sub's headlights did not show a bottom.

Captain Jack backed the sub up.

"Let's go see about that bigger object we spotted on the sonar earlier," he said.

It only took a few seconds to find our target. Near another pile of rocks was a metal-looking object. It almost looked like a safe.

"Let's pick it up," said Captain Jack. "We'll have to take it to the surface to see what's inside."

There was a metal ring on top of the object. Captain Jack moved the sub's manipulator arm into place.

"Gotcha!" he said as the claw grabbed the ring. "Oh, but you're heavy, I see. Almost to the limit of what we can carry."

All of us held our breath listening to Captain Jack's one-sided conversation. He talked to his newfound treasure like it was alive. There was something both weird and comforting in how he did it.

"Let's take *Jacques* up so we can see what's in this box," Captain Jack ordered. "I'm sure this is going to be an interesting find!"

I looked at Isabella. Could it possibly be something from the *San Luis Pedro*? I could tell she was as excited as I was.

Jacques was slowly rising toward the surface when all of a sudden there was a tug on the sub. Then a grinding sound pierced our headphones and the sub jerked to a stop. Warning sounds rang out and red lights started flashing on our monitors.

Captain Jack sprang into action, moving several controls in repeated tests. But he couldn't get the sub to move. The propellers wouldn't respond. And with the heavy box held by the manipulator arm weighing them down, *Jacques* was starting to sink. There was a sickening sound as *Jacques* settled on the very top of the pile of rocks near the trench.

Then we heard Captain Jack's voice. He sounded professional. But tense.

"Bridge, we've got a problem. Over."

"Roger that, Captain Jack," Ben responded. "Can you tell what's happened?"

"I think we've sucked in some rope and it's wrapped around our propellers. We can't move."

I held my breath, hearing "and that's final" in my head. *What does this mean?*

Captain Jack continued.

"It gets worse. I need to release the metal box from the manipulator arm. It's too heavy and weighing us down. But the mechanism jammed when we stalled out. And I can't release it."

Isabella sucked in her breath.

"Oh, no, Uncle Jack," she whispered.

Captain Jack continued. "We've settled on top of a ridge of rocks over a trench. If we tip over with this weight and can't get the props going, we might keep sinking. And we have no idea how deep this trench may be."

I looked at Isabella. Her wide eyes and shocked look scared me.

"Isabella, tell them to get out of there," I urgently whispered.

She was shaking her head. "They can't exit the sub and scuba back to the surface. They're too deep. The water pressure would crush them."

"Well, then they need to untangle the rope!" I practically yelled.

That's my brother down there!

"They can't untangle the rope on their own, Marena," Isabella said. She put her hand on my shoulder to try to calm me. "And I've got my hands full flying *Flipper*. I'm going to need some help."

Captain Jack's voice came over the headphones. I had forgotten that he and Lucas could hear everything we were saying.

"Isabella's right, Marena. You and *Flipper* need to untangle the rope from our props and cut the metal box loose."

I looked at Isabella—confused.

Wait. What?

Isabella looked at me and nodded her head.

Then I got it.

Isabella could fly the ROV into position, but she would need me to manipulate the arms to set *Jacques* free.

Not me! I'm not experienced enough!

Isabella saw my panic.

"You have to try," she said. "There is enough oxygen to keep them safe for days. But if the sub tips into the trench, they could fall deeper than the sub may be able to handle."

It took a moment for her words to sink in.

"You mean," I asked slowly, "Captain Jack and Lucas could ..."

I can't say it out loud!

"Ray-Ray," Lucas's voice broke the silence. "Remember what you learned on the *OceanXplorer*. Colin said always prepare for the unexpected—"

I finished the sentence for him. "—and when it happens, don't panic. Just think your way through it."

"That's right," he replied. "We've got to think our way through this!"

The next thing I heard was Ben's voice coming from the bridge.

"I've radioed for help," he said. "The Coast Guard

is on standby for flight assistance. And the *OceanXplorer* said they are on their way."

"Good," Isabella said. "The *OceanXplorer*'s subs can go deeper than ours."

That made me feel better. But her next words did not.

Isabella turned to me and placed both hands on my shoulders. She looked me directly in the eyes.

"Our biggest problem, Marena, is that we don't know how much time we have. So even though we have help on the way, we're going to have to take action now."

I stared back at her, not wanting to say what I was thinking.

What if I make a mistake?

She didn't take her eyes off mine. I could feel her willing me to find my courage.

"You really think I can do this?" I asked in a shaky voice.

Before Isabella could answer, I heard Lucas reply.

"Yes, you can," he said with confidence.

Then he said something in a much quieter voice that sent shivers of fear down my spine.

"You have to, Ray-Ray. You may be our only hope."

CHAPTER 10
DISCOVERING TRUE TREASURE

Isabella was expertly guiding *Flipper* close to *Jacques'* extended manipulator arm. I liked thinking about the ROV and the sub with their own names. It made it seem like we had a bigger team to help.

I sat in the co-pilot's seat, tightly holding the controls to *Flipper*'s manipulator arms in my lap.

No way am I going to let Lucas down!

A crackle came over my headset. Second Officer Ben said something like "Patching through now." Then I heard a familiar voice.

"Marena, this is Colin from the *OceanXplorer*. Do you copy? Over."

"Colin! Yes, I copy!" I practically shouted into the microphone.

"*Jacques* is all jammed and tangled and I have to try to use *Flipper*'s manipulator arms to set them free. But I'm really scared I'm not going to be able to do it and they're going to sink into the abyss!" I blurted out all at once.

"Yes, I know," Colin said. "And I also know you can do this, Marena. You are the best young co-pilot I've ever seen. A real natural."

His voice sounded calm and clear and reassuring as he continued to talk.

"We're on our way to help, but I'm also going to be right with you on this call to answer any questions you may have."

I breathed a sigh of relief. I would take any help I could get.

"Just remember how we practiced," he said. "Try to keep a light touch, and don't overcorrect. You don't want the manipulator arm to accidentally push the sub."

I never thought about that!

The idea that one misstep on my part could send my brother and Captain Jack into the deep trench was terrifying.

Isabella's voice brought me back to the present before I could panic any more.

"All right, *Flipper* is in position," she said.

As I stared through the murky water, I could see that the sub was tipped slightly forward due to the weight of the heavy box. Its headlights were pointed into the trench.

Jacques seemed to be warning me—just one false move, and we're going down there.

I tried to swallow, but my mouth was suddenly too dry.

"Okay, Marena," Captain Jack said. "Let's start with the propellers. What do you see?"

As Isabella inched *Flipper* closer to the sub, its lights shone directly on the propellers. We could see the rope.

"You were right, Captain Jack," I answered. "There is rope tangled in both props."

Isabella told me to extend the manipulator arms. I carefully did as she said.

"This one looks easiest," she said as she moved closer to one side. "Let's tackle it first."

The light of the ROV lit up one propeller. I moved

the manipulator arm toward it.

"Breathe, Marena," Colin said in a low voice.

How did he know I was holding my breath?

I inhaled deeply and blew the air out, then shrugged my shoulders to get rid of the tension. As I moved the arm in closer, I zoned out on everything else. The manipulator claw felt like it was my own hand. All I had to do was cut that annoying piece of rope away.

I made one cut, then another, slowly snipping away at the tangled mess.

As pieces came free, the rope loosened. I gave a tug at one long piece and the waterlogged rope just floated away.

"Excellent!" Isabella said as she flew the ROV back just a bit. "One down, one to go."

"Good work, Marena," Colin said. I closed my eyes in relief. But only for a second.

The next prop looked more tangled. Isabella got *Flipper* as close as she could. I extended an arm and went in for the cut.

But the rope was too knotted. I couldn't get a good grip. So I tried to move the arm in sideways.

Big mistake!

"Pull back, Marena," Isabella warned just as the arm clanked on the metal part of the prop.

It was a pretty hard hit. The submersible groaned and shifted.

"Colin!" I yelled. "What do I do?"

"Just stop, Marena," he answered. "Let it settle again. Don't move or make waves."

We all held our breaths.

The sub didn't move any more.

Captain Jack said in a low voice, "Lucas, I want you to stay very still."

I felt like I was going to cry. Another bump like that and they would surely go over.

"Try again, Marena," Captain Jack said. "You'll do it this time."

"And that's final" rang in my ears. How I hoped Captain Jack was right.

"Try going in from underneath and cut from the back," Isabella advised.

"But then I can't see what I'm cutting," I worried.

"No, Isabella's right," Colin said. "It doesn't matter if you can't see it. You will tell by the feel that it's the soft rope."

I took another deep breath and gently moved my clawlike hand underneath the prop and up toward the rope. Colin was right. I could tell by the feel when I hit the rope. I gently opened and closed the claw, trying to cut my way through.

The minutes felt like hours. I didn't know if I was making progress. Then, suddenly, the claw cut through. The rope started to float free. There was a small clank on the prop as I moved the arm back as quickly as I dared. I grabbed an end of the loose rope and gently tugged it free.

"Marena did it!" Isabella cried as she backed the ROV away.

Before anyone could respond, Captain Jack's voice boomed a loud warning.

"Don't move, Lucas!"

We all froze at the tone of his voice.

"We have to get rid of this weight," Captain Jack said in a softer voice. "Even if the props restart, the weight could still sink us."

The Captain was right. Just because the rope was free didn't mean the sub was safe. The metal box was still a problem.

Colin spoke up. "The *OceanXplorer* is twenty minutes out, Captain. If you can hold your position, our submersible will hook a cable to you before you try the props."

"Good idea, Colin," Captain Jack replied. "That way, maybe we can save the artifact we're holding."

It sounded like the safest plan. We all glanced at the time. Twenty minutes wasn't too long to wait.

But you have to expect the unexpected.

For no reason we could see, the sub suddenly started to tilt. That small motion caused some rocks to give way. We stared in horror as the little sub began to slip forward toward the trench.

Isabella flew *Flipper* to the front of the sub.

"Marena, do you see how *Jacques'* claw is locked onto the metal ring of the box?" she asked. "You need to cut through that ring. Then the box will fall away."

I followed her directions and positioned *Flipper's* claw to make the powerful cut. Nobody said it. But we all thought it. A box that may even have belonged to the *San Luis Pedro* was going to sink down into the trench—and we would never know what treasure it might hold.

The rocks shifted a bit more.

"Just do it!" Isabella ordered. Her voice was loud and clear.

I made the cut. The sub jerked up slightly when the box came free. We watched the box disappear into the deep.

"Starting thrusters!" Captain Jack yelled as he pushed on his controls.

The props turned and sputtered, struggling to start.

Lucas!

Marena!

I swore I heard my brother's voice calling my name inside my own head.

Then I heard something else. It was the soft whir of the propellers as they started to spin. *Jacques* was under power again and its headlights were pointed up toward the surface.

A cheer erupted from all of us, Colin included.

I fell back into my seat. The relief made me feel too weak to stand.

"Ray-Ray, you did it!" Lucas cried. His strong and happy voice sounded like music to my ears. I could think of only one thing: Prepare for the unexpected.

And when it happens, just think it through. I knew I had let one treasure go to save the most important one of all.

"This is one mighty impressive research ship," Captain Jack said. You could hear the respect in his voice.

We were all back on board the *OceanXplorer*, sitting in Mission Control. Colin had done a sonar exploration of the trench. The bottom was at 5,000 meters, far deeper than what *Jacques* could have safely handled.

A wide sweep using the *OceanXplorer* sonar showed no more signs of the *San Luis Pedro* wreck. The anchor chain seemed to be from a more recent wreck. It was probably the cargo ship that Captain Jack had originally set out to find.

Lucas was eager to get back to his internship. And I was finally ready to fly home, although I did hate the idea of telling Aisha that the hunt for the *San Luis Pedro* was over.

She'll say, "Only for the time being!"

"Wait. Colin, did you see it?" Anna suddenly asked.

Colin was flying *Chimaera* over the rocky area where Captain Jack had found the anchor chain.

We all looked up at the screen. A very large creature floated into view. It was tube-shaped with tentacles at one end. It wrapped itself around a manipulator arm—almost like it was posing for the camera.

"What is it?" I asked.

"It's a giant squid!" Captain Jack yelled. "I've never seen one before. Can you believe it? It must be bigger than me!"

The whole crew was laughing excitedly.

"Do you know how rare it is to see one of these guys?" Anna asked. I had never heard her sound so thrilled. It was as if she had just been given a really valuable gift.

As Lucas and I watched the celebration, we both knew we were seeing something special.

"You starting to understand treasure hunting yet?" he asked.

"Maybe a little," I answered, looking at the happy crew. "But I still think it would've been cool to find a treasure chest loaded with jewels and gold!"

"Copy that!" he agreed with a laugh.

"But seriously, Marena," he said in a suddenly

sincere tone of voice. "I think what you did with *Flipper* was amazing. I mean, you actually saved my life. I owe you."

Tears sprang to my eyes.

You'd do exactly the same for me.

I struggled for control. I really didn't want to start blubbering in front of everyone.

But wait a minute. What was that last thing Lucas said?

"Hey," I said as I blinked away my tears. "You're right, Lucas! You do owe me—BIG-TIME."

He only cringed a bit.

"Yeah, well, we'll talk about it," he answered as he put his arm around me in a brotherly squeeze, steering me toward the door. "But remember that time I saved you from that big kid who was picking on you?"

I laughed at Lucas's attempt to even the score. This negotiation was going to be fun. And as I felt the weight of his arm on my shoulders, I knew one thing for certain. The most important treasure of all had nothing to do with money. And at that moment, I was the richest kid on the planet.

THE END

THE OCEANX MISSION

TO EXPLORE THE OCEAN AND BRING IT BACK TO THE WORLD

This book, *Danger in the Deep Sea*, is a fun, fictional story. But guess what? The OceanX mission and the *OceanXplorer* ship are real! Turn the page to learn more about this very exciting and important mission to explore and protect the oceans.

The *OceanXplorer* has a landing pad for its very own helicopter.

VERY COOL TECH!

The *Nadir* can explore to about 1,000 meters (3,300 feet) below the surface—much deeper than humans can dive on their own.

The *OceanXplorer* is nearly the length of a football field—and for good reason. Besides laboratories and living quarters for the crew, the ship carries two underwater submersibles, named *Nadir* and *Neptune*. These subs can each take three people on a dive and are loaded with lights, cameras, and science equipment. Imagine cruising in one of the subs, looking through the dome at the wonderful underwater world all around you!

We mustn't forget about the *OceanXplorer's* two remotely operated vehicles, or ROVs! These don't carry people but are connected to the ship by cable so that the pilots on board the *OceanXplorer* can "fly" them wherever they need them to go.

The ROVs can go much deeper than the subs to reveal some of the darkest corners of the ocean using their powerful lights. Their robotic arms can collect samples from way down below for the scientists waiting in the labs above.

The *Chimaera* ROV can take samples from the ocean floor at 6,000 meters (over 19,000 feet)—that's nearly four miles below the surface!

MEET REAL-LIFE OCEANX CREW MEMBERS

Andrew Craig is a ROV pilot, like Colin in the story.

ANDREW CRAIG is a subsea technology specialist and expert ROV pilot. Even though he grew up on a farm in Ireland, it didn't take him long to find the sea. After college, he became a diving instructor, and he's been enjoying underwater adventures ever since. Andrew loves the teamwork it takes to guide the ROV in getting the best results for each scientist's mission. He also enjoys the thrill of discovering something for the first time.

TRIVIA Andrew has worked on teams that have discovered and explored real long-lost shipwrecks.

Jessie Boulton is a navigation expert.

JESSIE BOULTON is a Second Officer on board the *OceanXplorer*. This means she often takes control of the ship for the captain, just as Ben did for Captain Jack in the story. It takes years to learn how to steer a ship the size of the *OceanXplorer*. The training includes learning to firefight and how to survive in the water in case of an emergency.

Jessie grew up on the English coast and has always loved the sea. She is really excited about OceanX's mission. Jessie also says her job gives her the perfect view. When she's on the ship's bridge, she can look all around at the open ocean. At the same time, she can watch a live ROV video screen that shows her what's going on thousands of feet below the surface.

TRIVIA Jessie can drive the *OceanXplorer* forward, backward, and sideways, and can even spin it in circles if the captain orders it.

COOL DISCOVERIES OCEANX IS MAKING

SURPRISING SQUID

Just like the characters in this book, OceanX explorers never know what they're going to find next. As the OceanX team was exploring a shipwreck in the Red Sea using the ROV, they got a big surprise. While they were watching the ROV's live video footage of the dive, a very large and strange-looking creature swam into view. OceanX later confirmed that what they had seen was the giant form of the purpleback flying squid. It looked about six feet long.

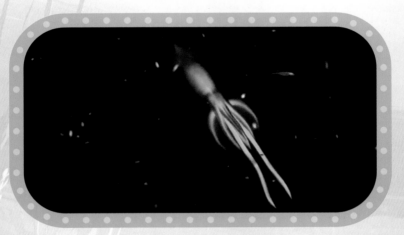

The giant purpleback flying squid looks like an alien creature in the underwater light.

The ROV's video footage shows the squid making itself at home in the shipwreck.

It's really rare to spot such a large purpleback flying squid! But the story gets even more interesting. When the OceanX team went back to the Red Sea a few years later, they ran into the same species at the same location. So it's possible that some purpleback squid have now made the shipwreck their new home.

MEET THE AUTHOR

Kate Jerome is an award-winning author who has written hundreds of science books for kids, including many about ocean conservation. In fact, the very first book she ever wrote was published by the Monterey Bay Aquarium.

Kate currently serves as a Director Emeritus on the South Carolina Aquarium's board. She is also an adviser to the national Reading Partners organization and an active alumna and mentor at Stanford University's Distinguished Careers Institute.

Just like her character Marena, Kate loves to ask questions—particularly if they result in meaningful conversations between generations!

TRIVIA

In *Danger in the Deep Sea*, Kate named Captain Jack's submersible *Jacques* in honor of the famous French oceanographer Jacques Cousteau.

READ MORE OCEANX ADVENTURES!